OLIVER
and the
OIL SPILL

OLIVER
and the
OIL SPILL

written and illustrated by
ARUNA CHANDRASEKHAR

LANDMARK EDITIONS, INC.

P.O. Box 4469 • 1402 Kansas Avenue • Kansas City, Missouri 64127

(816) 241-4919

Dedicated to
Mother Earth

COPYRIGHT © 1991 BY ARUNA CHANDRASEKHAR

International Standard Book Number: 0-933849-33-8 (LIB.BDG.)

Library of Congress Cataloging-in-Publication Data
Chandrasekhar, Aruna, 1981-
    Oliver and the oil spill / written and illustrated by Aruna Chandrasekhar.
    p.   cm.
    Summary: Young Oliver and his mother are among a group of sea otters res-
cued from an oil spill.
    ISBN 0-933849-33-8 (lib. bdg.)
    [1. Otters — Juvenile fiction.   2. Otters — Fiction.
    3. Wildlife rescue — Fiction.   4. Wildlife conservation — Fiction.]
    I. Title.
    PZ10.3.C371501   1991   [E] — dc20   91-3340
                                                        CIP
                                                        AC

Editorial Coordinator: Nancy R. Thatch
Creative Coordinator: David Melton
Consultant: Ken Hill, D.V.M., Cordova, Alaska

Printed in the United States of America

Landmark Editions, Inc.
P.O. Box 4469
1402 Kansas Avenue
Kansas City, Missouri 64127
(816) 241-4919

OLIVER AND THE OIL SPILL

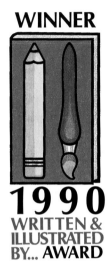

When Aruna Chandrasekhar read reports about a major oil spill that had killed thousands of sea otters, fish and birds, she was so disturbed and touched that she decided to write a book about a sea otter pup caught in an oil spill.

By singling out one otter pup as the central character, Aruna has created a very personal story. She was wise in not attempting to transform any of the animals into talking cartoon characters who think like human beings. Instead, they are allowed to react as animals. They know something is wrong, but they don't know what has happened to make the water look and smell strange. They are aware that fish and birds are dying and all the otters are becoming very ill, but they don't understand why. They realize they are trapped by something, but they don't know what it is or how to combat it.

Aruna's sensitive story will interest young readers, who will relate to the seriousness of the situation and be reminded of the importance of protecting Earth's environment. Aruna's fine illustrations provide visual beauty and add to the impact of her narrative. Her splendid choices of colors are perfect for the changing moods of her story.

We at Landmark thoroughly enjoyed working with Aruna in all phases of the final production of her book. She is a very industrious young lady. She never complained about the amount of work required to complete her illustrations or having to make necessary revisions in her text. Aruna was always enthusiastic and eager to improve her book.

Aruna knows how important it is to protect the delicate balance of life on our planet. Her story of OLIVER AND THE OIL SPILL offers a gentle plea for us to consider and attend to the environmental problems that threaten the well being of all living things.

— David Melton
Creative Coordinator
Landmark Editions, Inc.

Oliver was a sea otter pup who lived in the ocean. He and his mother were part of a large group of otters called a *raft*.

Every day Oliver and the other pups splashed about and played in the water. They liked to swim among the leafy stalks of kelp that grew up from the ocean floor.

The mother otters stayed busy too. They dived many times
to the bottom of the ocean to hunt for shellfish to eat.

Before the mothers dived, they always wrapped long
strands of kelp around their pups. They did not want the
pups to drift away and get lost in the big ocean.

Every day Oliver's mother showed him how to dive deeper and deeper into the water.

"I don't think I'll ever be able to swim to the bottom," Oliver said.

"Yes, you will," his mother told him. "One day you will be big enough and strong enough to go all the way down and find your own food."

Oliver's mother dived for many kinds of shellfish—clams, crabs, abalone and sea urchins. She usually returned to the surface with a shellfish in one paw and a rock in the other.

Oliver liked to watch his mother open shellfish. As she floated on her back, she would place a rock on her chest and hit the shell against it.

"Watch carefully," his mother often told him. "One day you will have to crack the shells yourself to get to the meat inside."

After every meal Oliver's mother carefully cleaned her fur and Oliver's too.

"You must always keep your fur clean," she told him. "If it gets dirty, you won't stay warm or be able to float on top of the water."

"Would I sink to the bottom of the ocean?" Oliver asked.

"Yes," his mother answered, "and you couldn't swim back up and get air."

"We have to breathe air to live, don't we?" Oliver asked.

"That's right," his mother replied.

10

Each night Oliver slept against his mother's warm chest. They were surrounded by the other otters, all wrapped in strands of kelp. As the raft of otters floated together on the rolling waves, Oliver always felt safe.

But one night while the otters slept, something terrible happened. Several miles away a ship crashed against a jagged rock. The rock cut a large hole in the ship's side.

The ship was a big oil tanker. Gallons of black oil started pouring from the hole. Soon the oil spread across the surface of the water and moved toward the shore.

The next morning Oliver's mother suddenly awakened.
"What's the matter?" he asked.

"Something is wrong," she replied. "The water smells very strange."

His mother became more upset when she saw dead fish floating on the ocean. The other otters were worried too.

"What happened to the fish?" Oliver asked.

"I don't know," his mother answered.

The next day the otters were awakened by squawking birds. Many of the birds were running frantically about on the beach. Their feathers were covered with black oil, and they couldn't fly very well.

"What's wrong with the birds?" Oliver asked.

"I don't know," his mother answered.

Soon a group of people came to the beach. They started catching the birds and carrying them away in boxes. Oliver wondered where they were taking the birds.

After a while Oliver's mother began to dive for shellfish. She brought up a clam, cracked it open, and gave it to Oliver.

He took one bite, then stopped. "This clam doesn't taste very good," he said.

"I know," his mother replied. "But you must have food. So try to eat it anyway."

The following morning there were more dead fish. And more sick birds had gathered on the beach. Now the thick black oil was spreading across the top of the water.

"This stuff makes my fur sticky!" Oliver complained.

"I will clean it off," his mother told him. And she tried to lick Oliver's fur clean, but more and more globs of oil kept sticking to his coat.

"This stuff is making me sick," Oliver said.

"I'm sick, too," his mother replied, "and so are many of the other otters."

As more oil covered their coats, the otters grew colder and weaker. When their fur became too matted with oil, many of them sank into the water. Oliver noticed they didn't come back up for air.

During the night Oliver and his mother managed to stay afloat. But by morning even more oil had covered the water. Most of the otters were now very sick. The pups were crying, and their mothers didn't know how to help them.

Before long the otters heard the sound of motors. When the motorboats came near, people threw nets into the water and began to catch the otters.

Oliver and his mother were frightened. They tried to escape, but they were too sick to swim away. Soon Oliver was caught in a net and pulled onto a boat. His mother would not leave him, so she was caught too.

"What are they going to do to us?" Oliver asked.

"I don't know," his mother replied. "But don't worry, little one. We are together."

When the boat stopped, Oliver and his mother were taken to the Wildlife Rescue Center. Inside the building, people were trying to wash the oil off the otters.

The people were gentle and friendly, but the otters were frightened. They were not used to being handled by humans.

The people gave the otters injections. That helped the animals relax and sleep while they were being bathed.

When it was Oliver's turn to have a bath, he was placed in a tub of warm water. He didn't like the smell of the soap, and he certainly didn't like being stuck with a needle.

But when Oliver woke up after his bath, he was one happy otter. It felt so good to have his fur clean again.

Then Oliver looked around for his mother. The people were bathing her now.

"They will get your fur clean too," he called to her. "Then you will feel much better."

But his mother did not reply.

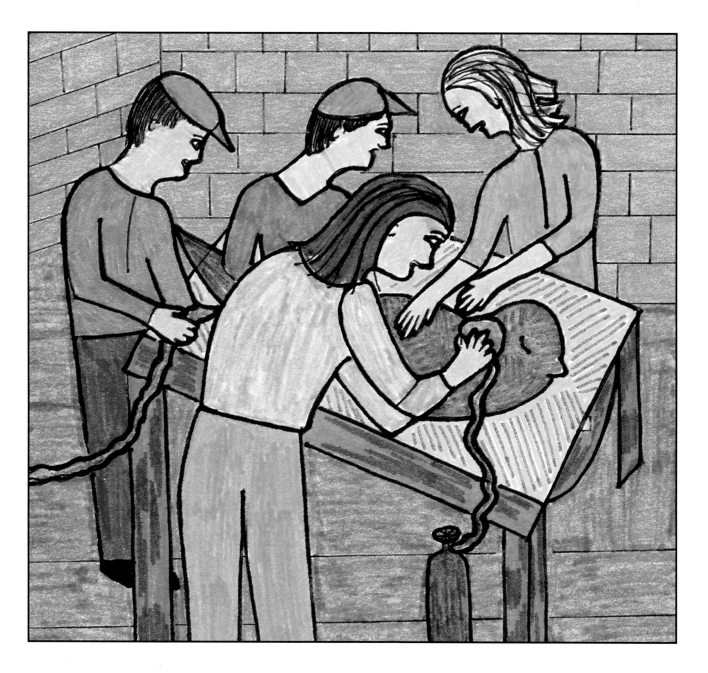

Suddenly the people became very excited. Oliver could see they were concerned about his mother.

"She's not breathing!" one of them said.

They quickly grabbed an oxygen mask and put it over the otter's face. Then they started pushing on her chest. The people worked for some time, but they could not get her to breathe.

Then Oliver watched as the people gently lifted his mother from the tub. As they carried her out of the room, Oliver's eyes filled with tears. Somehow he knew he would never see his mother again.

During the months that followed, the people gave Oliver plenty of shellfish to eat. They let him swim with the other otters in a big tank too. That was fun. But Oliver was almost one year old — a yearling — and he wanted to be back in the ocean.

One morning Oliver and another otter were put in boxes and carried to a boat. The otters were frightened. They didn't like the sound of the boat's motor. Oliver wondered where the man was taking them now.

The boat sped across the water. When it finally stopped, the man helped the otters into the ocean.

"I'm home!" Oliver exclaimed.

He was so happy! He splashed in the water and darted about in the kelp.

But when Oliver calmed down, he noticed there were not many otters left in the ocean. All the little pups were gone. A large number of adult otters had not survived either.

Oliver missed his mother most of all.

The other otters began to dive for shellfish. But none of them offered to share their food with Oliver. Then he remembered what his mother had told him: "One day you will have to dive for your own food."

Oliver didn't know if he would be able to dive to the bottom of the ocean. But he knew he had to try.

He took a deep breath and dived under the water. Down, down he went. Although he swam deeper than he ever had before, he could not reach the bottom. He had to hurry back to the top for air.

Then Oliver tried again. He swam even farther down into the ocean. Still he could not reach the bottom. Once more he had to return to the top.

By now he was really hungry and beginning to feel weak. He had to have food! This time he was determined to go all the way down.

After taking a deeper breath, Oliver swam down, down, and down to the darkest depths. It was so dark, he could not see anything.

At last he touched the sandy floor of the ocean. Wasting no time, he began to search with his paws. When he finally felt a hard shell, he grabbed it and held it tightly.

Air! He had to have air! But Oliver would not let himself swim back to the top until he got a rock. Then up, up, up he went, up into the light. His head popped out of the water, and he gasped for air.

Then Oliver rolled over onto his back. He placed the rock on his chest, just as his mother had taught him. He hit the shell against the rock. But the shell didn't crack. He hit it harder. It still didn't crack. So he raised the shell as high as he could and brought it down against the rock with all his might.

Crack! The shell split open. Oliver had finally done it! And he happily ate his first catch.

Oliver wished his mother could see him now. He knew she would be so proud of him.

Then Oliver flipped over in the water and dived straight down to search for another shellfish.

The Big Oil Spill
by Aruna Chandrasekhar

On March 24, 1989, the giant oil tanker, *Exxon Valdez,* strayed off course and entered shallow water. Sharp rocks gashed open the tanker's steel hull. Almost 11 million gallons of oil spilled into the Pacific Ocean along the coast of Alaska. It was the worst oil spill in the history of the United States.

The released oil killed thousands of fish, sea animals and seabirds. Many types of underwater plants were damaged too. The full amount of damage done to the ocean's environment will never be known.

It is certain that at least 1,000 sea otters died. But some scientists suspect that more than 3,000 were killed. Many land animals and birds were harmed too. Grizzly bear, foxes, caribou, gray wolves, and bald eagles died after eating fish and birds that had been killed by the poison oil.

About 12,000 people helped in trying to clean the water and the beaches. But they could not remove all of the oil. After two years the oil still oozes up from the ocean floor, and it can be found under rocks and in the ground. Scientists who study oil spills believe it will take ten to twenty years for the environment to overcome the damage the oil caused.

Scientists are working to find better ways to clean up spilled oil. But the best way to keep the oceans and beaches clean is to stop the oil spills before they happen. Many concerned people are trying to get better safety laws passed so tankers will be built stronger and their crews will have to be more careful.

THE NATIONAL WRITTEN & ILLUSTRATE

— THE 1989 NATIONAL AWARD WINNING BOOKS —

Lauren Peters
age 7

Michael Cain
age 11

Problems at the North Pole — written & illustrated by Lauren Peters

the Legend of SIR MIGUEL — written and illustrated by MICHAEL CAIN

WE ARE A THUNDERSTORM — written and photographed by amity gaige

Amity Gaige
age 16

—THE 1987 NATIONAL AWARD WINNING BOOKS—

JOSHUA DISOBEYS — Written and Illustrated by Dennis Vollmer

THE HALF & HALF DOG — written and illustrated by LISA GROSS

WHO OWNS THE SUN? — written & illustrated by STACY CHBOSKY

Dennis Vollmer
age 6

Lisa Gross
age 12

—THE 1989 GOLD AWARD WINNERS—

BROKEN ARROW BOY — WRITTEN and ILLUSTRATED BY ADAM MOORE and his friends

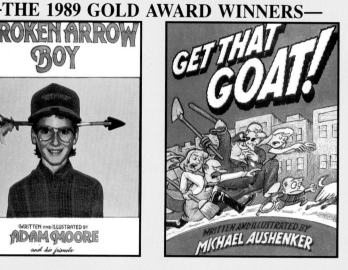

GET THAT GOAT! — WRITTEN AND ILLUSTRATED BY MICHAEL AUSHENKER

Students' Winning Books Motivate and Inspire

Each year it is Landmark's plea
sure to publish the winning books o
The National Written & Illustrate
By… Awards Contest For Student
These are important books because the
supply such positive motivation an
inspiration for other talented student
to write and illustrate books too!

Students of All Ages Love the Winning Books

Students of all ages enjoy readin
these fascinating books created by ou
young author/illustrators. When stu
dents see the beautiful books, printe
in full color and handsomely bound i
hardback covers, they, too, will be
come excited about writing and illus
trating books and eager to enter them
in the Contest.

Enter Your Book In the Next Contest

If you are 6 to 19 years of ag
you may enter the Contest too. Pe
haps your book may be one of the ne
winners and you will become a pu
lished author and illustrator too.

Stacy Chbosky
age 14

Adam Moore
age 9

Michael Aushenker
age 19

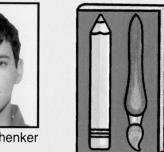

— THE 1988 NATIONAL AWARD WINNING BOOKS —

Leslie Ann MacKeen
age 9

—THE 1986 NATIONAL AWARD WINNING BOOKS—

Elizabeth Haidle
age 13

Heidi Salter
age 19

— THE 1985 GOLD AWARD WINNERS —

Winners Receive Contracts, Royalties and Scholarships

The National Written & Illustrated by... Contest Is an Annual Event! There is no entry fee! The winners receive publishing contracts, royalties on the sale of their books, and all-expense-paid trips to our offices in Kansas City, Missouri, where professional editors and art directors assist them in preparing their final manuscripts and illustrations for publication.

Winning Students Receive Scholarships Too! The R.D. and Joan Dale Hubbard Foundation will award a total of $30,000 in scholarship certificates to the winners and the four runners-up in all three age categories. Each winner receives a $5,000 scholarship; those in Second Place are awarded a $2,000 scholarship; and those in Third, Fourth, and Fifth Places receive a $1,000 scholarship.

To obtain Contest Rules, send a self-addressed, stamped, business-size envelope to: THE NATIONAL WRITTEN & ILLUSTRATED BY... AWARDS CONTEST FOR STUDENTS, Landmark Editions, Inc., P.O. Box 4469, Kansas City, MO 64127.

Amy Hagstrom
age 9

Isaac Whitlatch
age 11

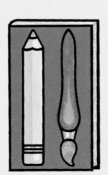

Karen Kerber
age 12

David McAdoo
age 14

Dav Pilkey
age 19

THE WRITTEN & ILLUSTRATED BY... CONTEST
— THE 1990 NATIONAL AWARD WINNING BOOKS —

Aruna Chandrasekhar
age 9

Anika Thomas
age 13

Cara Reichel
age 15

Jonathan Kahn
age 9

Jayna Miller
age 19

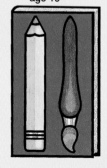

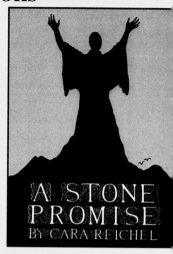

— THE 1990 GOLD AWARD WINNERS —

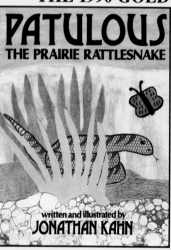

Winning the Gold Award and having my book published are two of the most exciting things that have ever happened to me! If you are a student between 6 and 19 years of age, and you li[k]e to write and draw, then create a book of your own and enter it in the Contest. Who knows? Maybe your book will be one o[f] the next winners, and you will become a published author and illustrator too.

— Jayna Miller
Author and Illustrator
TOO MUCH TRICK OR TREA[T]

To Help Students Create Amazing Books!

Written & Illustrated by...
by David Melton

This highly acclaimed teacher's manual offers classroom-proven, step-by-step instruction in all aspects of teaching students how to write, illustrate and bind original books. Contains suggested lesson plans and more than 200 illustrations. Loaded with information and positive approaches that really work.

... an exceptional book! Just browsing through it stimulates excitement for writing.
> Joyce E. Juntune, Executive Director
> American Creativity Association

The results are dazzling!
> Children's Book Review Service, Inc.

A "how to" book that really works!
> Judy O'Brien, Teacher

This book should be in every classroom.
> Tacoma Review Service

Written & Illustrated by...

a revolutionary two-brain approach for teaching students how to write and illustrate amazing books

David Melton

ISBN: 0-933849-00-1